D0005451

The Post Office

◈◈◈

The Post Office

RABINDRANATH TAGORE

TRANSLATED BY KRISHNA DUTTA
AND ANDREW ROBINSON

INTRODUCTION BY ANITA DESAI

ILLUSTRATIONS BY

MICHAEL McCURDY

ST. MARTIN'S PRESS NEW YORK

We dedicate this translation to the memory of
Alex Aronson.

K.D. AND A.R.

Production Editor: David Stanford Burr
Book design by Gretchen Achilles

Library of Congress Cataloging-in-Publication Data

Tagore, Rabindranath, 1861–1941.
[Dakaghara. English]
The Post Office/by Rabindranath Tagore; translated by Krishna Dutta and Andrew Robinson; illustrations by Michael McCurdy.—1st ed.
p. cm.
ISBN 0-312-14703-1
I. Dutta, Krishna. II. Robinson, Andrew. III. McCurdy, Michael.
PK1722.A2D83 1996
891'.4443—dc20 96-8484
CIP

First Edition: September 1996
10 9 8 7 6 5 4 3 2 1

Contents

◈

Introduction vi

Translators' Preface ix

Dramatis Personae xii

The Post Office 1

Glossary 50

About the Author, Translators, and Illustrator 51

Introduction

◈

Rabindranath Tagore knew imprisonment as a child—the imprisonment of the spirit. One of his earliest memories was of a servant called Shyam who would "place me in a selected spot, trace a chalk line around me, and warn me with a solemn face and uplifted finger of the perils of transgressing this circle. Whether the danger was physical or mental I never fully understood, but fear certainly possessed me." Confined to the immense, gloomy family home in Calcutta, he could only gaze with longing at "this limitless thing called Outside, flashes, sounds and scents of which used to come and touch me through interstices. It seemed to want to beckon me through the shutters with a variety of gestures. But it was free and I was bound—there was no way of our meeting." In poem after poem he wrote of this sense of imprisonment, balanced by an instinctive awareness of the possibility of release: "Looking back at my childhood I feel the thought that recurred most often was that I was surrounded by mystery. Something undreamt of was lurking everywhere, and every day the uppermost question was: when, oh! when would I come across it?" This mystery was personified in his poetry by the bird that was free, or by a beautiful siren:

Someone singing is coming close to the shore.
I look and seem to know her.
The full sails pass,

She gives no glance . . .
*I look and seem to know her.**

Tagore's poetry has remained largely inaccessible to non-Bengali readers, and even more so the many hundreds of songs he composed. Of his entire literary oeuvre perhaps his little play *The Post Office* has had the most direct and powerful appeal to audiences across the world.

Here it is the child Amal who is confined indoors by sickness and his doctor's harsh prescription. Sitting at the window, he gazes out at what his imagination transforms into a magic glade. Beguiling figures—a kindly watchman, a fakir, a curdseller, some boys, and a flower girl, Shudha, appear—tell him about the hills and woods and riverbank where they wander and seem touched, and moved, by the boy's intense longing for the great world he thinks they know. He is given hope by the sight of the Raja's post office that seems to rise overnight outside his window, flying a golden flag; the watchman assures him that the Raja himself will soon be sending him a letter. Amal's longing for the vast and beautiful earth becomes intensified into his longing for that letter: It arrives, and he is freed.

Typically in Tagore's work, it is the child who is best prepared to meet this supreme experience of life—through his innocence, and his total lack of fear or prejudice. Enchanted by the very idea of time as a journey, he questions: "Where is time going? To what land?"

*"The Golden Boat," trans. Krishna Dutta and Andrew Robinson.

Watchman: Nobody knows that.

Amal: You mean nobody's been there? I would love to run away with time to this land that nobody knows.

Through Amal, Tagore expressed his conviction that life's cycle can only be completed and its full meaning grasped on reaching death. So light is his touch, so magical the manner in which his little play is presented, that it has bewitched audiences everywhere—not only those who looked to it for exotic diversion, but those who turned to it in times of their most dire need—Paris on the eve of its fall, Janusz Korczak when leading the children of the Warsaw ghetto into extinction.

In appearance the play is as modest as a dewdrop; in effect it is as profound as the ocean.

Anita Desai

Translators' Preface

◈

When Mahatma Gandhi saw this play, he wrote to a friend: "I was enraptured to witness *The Post Office* performed by the Poet and his company. Even as I dictate this, I seem to hear the exquisitely sweet voice of the Poet and the equally exquisite acting on the part of the sick boy . . . I did not have enough of it, but what I did have had a most soothing effect upon my nerves which are otherwise always on trial." William Butler Yeats, who first had the play produced in English and also wrote a preface to it, thought it a masterpiece and said: "On the stage the little play shows that it is very perfectly constructed, and conveys to the right audience an emotion of gentleness and peace."

Tagore wrote it in Bengal in 1911, not long after losing his son, his daughter, and his wife to disease. In the middle of the night, while lying under the stars on the roof of his house in Shantiniketan (the "Abode of Peace"), he had a strange experience. "My mind took wing. Fly! Fly!—I felt an anguish . . . There was a call to go somewhere and a premonition of death, together with intense emotion—this feeling of restlessness I expressed in writing *Dak Ghar [The Post Office]*." Soon afterward, Tagore's worldwide odyssey began.

Ten years on, having watched a German performance in Berlin (with the young Elisabeth Bergner playing the boy Amal), Tagore explained the play's intended meaning to an English friend, C. F. Andrews:

> *Amal represents the man whose soul has received the call of the open road . . . But there is the post office in front of his window, and Amal waits for the King's letter to come to him direct from the King, bringing him the message of emancipation. At last the closed gate is opened by the King's own physician, and that which is 'death' to the world of hoarded wealth and certified creeds brings him awakening in the world of spiritual freedom.*
>
> *The only thing that accompanies him in his awakening is the flower of love given to him by Shudha.*

Such was its universal appeal, *The Post Office* was translated into many European languages. Each artist coming to it has made it speak afresh to his own place and time in his own idiom (as witness Michael McCurdy's woodcuts). Its Spanish translator, the celebrated poet Juan Ramón Jiménez, wrote of "my hand that helped to give our Spanish form to the rhythm of Tagore's immense heart." In 1940, the evening before Paris fell to the Nazis, André Gide's French translation was read over the radio. And in 1942, in the Warsaw ghetto, a Polish version was the last play performed in the orphanage of Janusz Korczak. When, after the performance, Korczak was asked why he chose the play, he answered that "eventually one had to learn to accept serenely the angel of death." Within a month, he and his children were taken away and gassed.

Tagore's insight into death is perhaps at its deepest in this play. Discussing it with an Italian nobleman, who felt that the play was about death "as a kind of revelation of the divine," Rabindranath made this beautiful response, later read at the funeral of his American admirer Dorothy Whitney Elmhirst:

I have had so many experiences of loved ones who have died that I think I have come to know something about death, something perhaps of its deeper meaning. Every moment that I have spent at the death bed of some dear friend, I have known this, yet it is very difficult to describe how for me that great ocean of truth to which all life returns, can never suffer diminution by death . . . I see how the individual life comes back into the bosom of this ocean at the moment of death, I have felt too how great and fathomless this ocean is, yet how full it is of personality. For personality is ever flowing into it . . . It becomes instilled with personality. Yet this ocean seems as nothing, as neither light nor darkness, but as one great extension of the universe, an eternity of peace and life . . .

Science recognizes atoms, all of which can be weighed and measured, but never recognizes personality, the one thing that lies at the basis of reality. All creation is that, for apart from personality, there is no meaning in creation. Water is water to me, because I am I. And so I have felt that in this great infinite, in this ocean of personality, from which my own little personal self has sprung, lies the completion of the cycle, like those jets of water from a fountain which rise and fall and come back home again.

Dramatis Personae

◈

Madhav Dutta

Amal, a small boy and Madhav's adopted child

Doctor

Curdseller

Watchman

{ *Thakurda,* a wanderer
{ *Fakir*

Village headman, a bully

Shudha, a flower girl

Village boys

Raja's (King's) *Herald*

Raja's (King's) *Physician*

Act One

Madhav's house

Madhav Dutta: What a mess I'm in. Before he came, he meant nothing to me—I had no worries. Then he came here out of nowhere and filled my entire home; if he leaves me now, this house will no longer seem like my home. Doctor, do you think he will—

Doctor: If the child is fated for long life, then he shall have it, but it is written in the *Ayurveda* that—

Madhav: What? Please tell me!

Doctor: The scriptures say, "Bile and fever, palsy and phlegm all—"

Madhav: Stop, stop, please don't recite those *slokas*; they just make me more anxious. Tell me instead what must be done.

Doctor (taking snuff): Great care must be observed.

Madhav: That I know, but what kind of care? You must tell me.

Doctor: I have told you before: On no account should he be allowed out-of-doors.

Madhav: But he's so young! To keep him inside all day is really cruel.

Doctor: What choice do you have? The autumn sun and wind

are both like venom to the boy, for as the scriptures say, "In epilepsy, fever or wheezing fit, in jaundice or in swelling—"

Madhav: Enough, that's enough scripture. So we have to shut him indoors—is there really no other cure?

Doctor: None at all, for in the wind and the sun—

Madhav: Oh cease with your "this, that, and the other." Please, stop it—just tell me what I have to do. Your remedies are so harsh. The poor boy is already putting up with a lot without complaining—but it breaks my heart to see how your prescription makes him suffer further.

Doctor: The greater the suffering, the happier the outcome. As the great sage Chyabana says, "In medication as in good counsel, the bitterest remedy brings the speediest results." Well, I must be going, Mr. Dutta.

[he goes]

Thakurda enters

Madhav: Oh no, Thakurda's back! Looks like trouble.

Thakurda: Why? Why should a fellow like me scare you?

Madhav: Because you make children run wild.

Thakurda: You are not a boy, you have no child in your house, and you are past the age for running away—why do you worry?

Madhav: Because I have brought a child to the house.

Thakurda: Indeed!

Madhav: My wife wanted to adopt a boy.

Thakurda: I've known that for a long time, but I thought you didn't want to.

Madhav: You know, I was making a lot of money by hard work, and I used to think how terrible it would be if some boy turned up and wasted all my money without any effort. But this one has somehow charmed me so much that—

Thakurda: —that no wealth is too much for him. And you now feel that the more you spend, the merrier your money's fate.

Madhav: Before, I was addicted to making money—I couldn't help myself. But now my reward is the knowledge that whatever I earn will be his.

Thakurda: And where did you find him?

Madhav: He's a sort of nephew of my wife through some village connection. He lost his mother very early, poor boy. And just recently, he lost his father, too.

Thakurda: How sad! Maybe I could be of some help to him.

Madhav: The doctor says that he is so sick with fever that there isn't much hope. Now the only cure is somehow to keep him inside, away from the autumn sunshine and breezes. But you always come along and gaily lead children outside—that's why you scare me.

Thakurda: Yes, I admit it, I have become a free spirit, like the autumn sun and wind. But I also know how to play games indoors. Let me finish a few errands of mine, then I will make friends with this boy of yours.

[he goes]

Amal enters

Amal: Uncle!

Madhav: What is it, Amal?

Amal: Can't I even go out into the courtyard?

Madhav: No, Amal.

Amal: Look, over there, where Auntie is grinding lentils, there's a squirrel, balancing on its tail and munching the broken bits between its paws—can't I please go and see?

Madhav: No, my son.

Amal: I wish I could be a squirrel—Uncle, why can't I go out?

Madhav: The doctor says that if you go out, you will get ill.

Amal: How does the doctor know that?

Madhav: What do you mean, Amal? Of course he knows! He has read so many huge old books.

Amal: Does reading make you know everything?

Madhav: Of course! Don't you know?

Amal (with a sigh): I have not read a single book, so I guess I don't know anything.

Madhav: But you are just like the greatest of pundits—you know, they never leave their houses.

Amal: Don't they?

Madhav: No, they don't; how can they? They only sit and read books, and never glance in any other direction. Amal, young fellow, you, too, will become a pundit—you will sit and read all those books, and everyone will gaze at you in wonder.

Amal: No! Uncle, please no, I beg you, I don't want to be a pundit, I don't want to be one, Uncle.

Madhav: Why not, Amal! If I could have been a pundit, my life would have been totally different.

Amal: I want to see everything—everything there is to see.

Madhav: What are you talking about? See what?

Amal: Those faraway hills, for instance, which I can see from my window—I would so love to cross over them.

Madhav: What a crazy idea! Just like that, for nothing, on a whim, you want to cross those hills? You are not talking sense. Those hills stand up so tall because they are forbidding you to go beyond them—otherwise, why would stone have been piled upon stone to form such a huge heap?

Amal: Uncle, are you sure they are really forbidding us? To me, it looks like the earth is mute, and so she is raising up her hands toward the sky and calling us. Distant people sitting beside their windows in the heat of midday are also hearing the call. Don't the pundits hear it?

Madhav: They are not mad like you—they don't want to listen.

Amal: Yesterday, I met someone as mad as me.

Madhav: Really? Tell me.

Amal: There was a bamboo pole across one of his shoulders. At the top of it was tied a small bundle. He held a small brass pot in his left hand. There was an old pair of curly-toed slippers on his feet, and he walked along the path through the fields toward the hills. I called out, "Where are you going?" He said, "I don't know—wherever I happen to go." So I asked him, "Why are you going?" And he replied, "I'm seeking work." Uncle, does everybody have to seek work?

Madhav: Of course. People are always looking for work.

Amal: All right, I'll be like them and go searching for work, too.

Madhav: What if you seek and don't find?

Amal: I will keep on searching. When the man with the slippers walked away, I watched him from our doorway. Not far off, where the stream flows past the fig tree, he put his pole down and gently washed his feet. Then he opened his sack, took out some maize flour, kneaded it with water, and ate *chhatu*. When he was finished, he picked up the sack again and put it on his shoulder, hitched up his clothes, waded into the stream, and made his way across. I said to Auntie that I'm going to go to the stream sometime and eat *chhatu*.

Madhav: What did she say?

Amal: She said, "Get well first, then I myself will take you to the stream and feed you with *chhatu*." When will I get better?

Madhav: It won't be much longer, young fellow.

Amal: Not long? You know, as soon as I get well I must be off.

Madhav: Where to?

Amal: There are so many winding streams I want to dip my feet in. And at noontime, when everyone is resting behind shuttered doors, I want to walk and walk in search of work, farther and farther.

Madhav: All right, but first get better, then you—

Amal: You won't tell me to become a pundit, Uncle, will you?

Madhav: What will you become then?

Amal: I can't think of anything yet—I will tell you when I've thought.

Madhav: But you shouldn't talk to strangers like that.

Amal: I like strangers very much.

Madhav: What if one were to snatch you away?

Amal: That would be fun. But no one ever takes me away; everyone wants me to sit right here.

Madhav: I have some work to do, so I must go. But son, don't wander outside, all right?

Amal: I won't. But Uncle, you must let me sit here in this room next to the road.

[Madhav goes]

◈ *Act Two* ◈

Madhav's house

Curdseller: *Dai, dai,* good *dai!*

Amal: Daiwallah, Daiwallah, oh Daiwallah!

Curdseller: What do you want? To buy some *dai*?

Amal: How can I? I have no money.

Curdseller: What kind of child are you? If you're not buying, why are you wasting my time?

Amal: I just want to walk with you.

Curdseller: With me?

Amal: When I hear your cry in the distance, it makes me so restless.

Curdseller (unhitching his harness): Young fellow, what are you doing, sitting there like that?

Amal: The doctor's forbidden me to go outdoors, so I must sit here all day, every day.

Curdseller: You poor child. What's wrong?

Amal: I don't know. I haven't read any books, so I can't know what is the matter with me. Daiwallah, where do you come from?

Curdseller: I come from our village.

Amal: Your village. Is it far away?

Curdseller: Our village is at the foot of the Panchmura Hills, beside the Shamli River.

Amal: Panchmura Hills, Shamli River—I think I've seen your village, although I don't remember when.

Curdseller: You have been there? Have you been to the foot of the hills?

Amal: No, I've never been there. But I feel as if I have. Doesn't your village lie beneath some ancient sprawling trees, next to a red road?

Curdseller: You are right, son.

Amal: And there are cows grazing on the hillside.

Curdseller: Right again! In our village, cows do graze, yes indeed.

Amal: And women come to fetch water from the river and carry it in pitchers on their heads—and they wear red saris.

Curdseller: Yes, yes, that's it. All of our dairywomen come to the river for their water. But not all of them wear red saris. You must have visited the place sometime.

Amal: No, I assure you, I have never been there. As soon as the doctor lets me go out, will you take me to your village?

Curdseller: Of course I will, with pleasure.

Amal: Teach me how to sell *dai,* as you do—walking all those far-off roads with your harness across your shoulder.

Curdseller: But my son, why sell *dai*? You should read books and become a pundit.

Amal: No, no, I will never become a pundit. I will take some *dai* from your village beneath the old banyan tree beside the red road, and I will sell it in distant villages. How does your call go? "*Dai, dai,* good *dai!*" Teach me the tune, won't you, please?

Curdseller: Heavens! Is such a tune worth teaching?

Amal: Don't say that, I like it. You know when you hear a hawk shrieking high up in the sky, the cry gives you a strange feeling? Well, your distant call—which seems to float through the trees from some far bend in the road—has the same effect on me.

Curdseller: Son, please have a pot of my *dai*.

Amal: But I have no money.

Curdseller: It doesn't matter, don't mention money. I would be ever so pleased if you ate some of my *dai*.

Amal: Have I delayed you much?

Curdseller: No, not at all, son, it's no loss at all. For you have shown me the joy in selling *dai*.

[he goes]

Amal (chanting): Dai, dai, good *dai! Dai* from the dairies beside the Shamli River in the Panchmura Hills. *Dai—dai!* Every dawn the dairywomen milk the cows under the trees, and every evening they set the *dai*—and what *dai* it is! *Dai, dai, dai-i,* delicious *dai*! Ah, look, there's the watchman doing his rounds. Watchman, oh Watchman, won't you come and listen to me for just a minute?

Watchman enters

Watchman: What's all this shouting for? Aren't you afraid of me?

Amal: Why should I be afraid of you?

Watchman: What if I arrest you, take you away?

Amal: Where will you take me? Far away, over the hills?

Watchman: I might take you straight to the Raja!

Amal: To the Raja! Would you really?! But the doctor has forbidden me to go out. No one can take me anywhere. I must just sit here all day and night.

Watchman: Doctor's orders? Ah, I can see your face is quite pale. There are dark rings under your eyes. The veins are sticking out in both of your arms.

Amal: Are you going to sound your gong?

Watchman: The time is not yet right.

Amal: Some people say, "time flies," while others say that "time is not yet ripe." But if you strike your gong, won't the time be right?

Watchman: How so? I sound the gong only when the time is right.

Amal: I do like your gong. I love listening to it, especially at noon after everyone's eaten and my uncle has gone out somewhere to work and Auntie dozes off reading the *Ramayana*, and our small dog curls up into its tail in some shadow of the courtyard—then I hear your gong strike, *dhong dhong, dhong dhong dhong!* But why do you strike it?

Watchman: It tells everyone that time does not stand still, that time always moves onward.

Amal: Where is time going? To what land?

Watchman: Nobody knows that.

Amal: You mean nobody's been there? I would love to run away with time to this land that nobody knows.

Watchman: All of us will go there one day, young man.

Amal: Me, too?

Watchman: Of course.

Amal: But the doctor has forbidden me to go out.

Watchman: Someday perhaps the doctor will hold your hand and take you there.

Amal: No, you don't know him, all he does is keep me locked up here.

Watchman: But there is a greater doctor than he, a doctor who can set you free.

Amal: When will this Great Doctor come for me? I'm so tired of staying here.

Watchman: Shouldn't say such things, son.

Amal: But I have to sit here all the time never going out, doing as I am told, and when your gong goes *dhong dhong dhong* I feel so frustrated. Watchman—?

Watchman: What is it?

Amal: Over there, across the road, that big house with a flag on top, with lots of people going in and out of it—what is it?

Watchman: It's the new post office.

Amal: Post office? Whose post office?

Watchman: The Raja's, of course—who else could have a post office? *(aside)* He's a strange boy.

Amal: Do letters come to the post office from the Raja himself?

Watchman: Yes, of course. Someday, there may even be a letter addressed to you.

Amal: A letter with my name on it? But I am only a child.

Watchman: The Raja sends his littlest letters to children.

Amal: Really? When will I get my letter? And how do you know that he's going to write to me?

Watchman: Why else would he bother to set up a post office with a splendid golden flag outside your open window? *(aside)* But I rather like the boy.

Amal: When the Raja's letter comes, who will give it to me?

Watchman: The Raja has many messengers—surely you have seen them running about with gold badges pinned to their chests?

Amal: Where do they go?

Watchman: From door to door, country to country. *(aside)* The boy's questions really are amusing.

Amal: When I grow up, I want to be a Raja's messenger.

Watchman: Ha ha ha! A Raja's messenger! Now there's a responsible job. Come rain, come shine, among rich, among poor, wherever you are you must deliver your letters—it's a tremendous job!

Amal: Why are you smiling that way? It's the best job there could be. Oh, I don't mean that your job isn't good, too—you strike your gong during the heat of noon, *dhong dhong dhong,* and also in the dead of night—sometimes I suddenly wake up and find that the lamp has gone out and I hear a deep, dark *dhong dhong dhong*!

Watchman: Uh-oh, here comes the big boss—time to run. If he catches me chatting with you, he's sure to cause trouble.

Amal: Where's the boss, which one is he?

Watchman: Over there, way down the road. Don't you see his big umbrella—the one made of palm leaves—bobbing up and down?

Amal: Has the boss been appointed by the Raja?

Watchman: Oh no—he's been appointed by himself. But if you don't obey him, he'll cause endless difficulties—that's why people are afraid of him. Our Headman's entire job seems to be troublemaking, for everyone. So that's enough talk for today, time to leave. I'll be back tomorrow morning to bring you the news of the town.

[*he goes*]

Amal: If I receive a letter every day from the Raja, that would be wonderful. I'll sit here by the window and read them. Oh, but I don't know how to read. I wonder who could read them for me? Auntie reads *Ramayana*. Maybe she can read the Raja's writing. If nobody can read the letters, I'll keep them and read them all later, when I grow up. But what if the Raja's messengers don't know about me? Mr. Headman, oh dear Mr. Headman, could I talk to you for a minute?

Headman: Who's this? Bellowing at me in the road! Who's this monkey?

Amal: You are the Headman. I hear that everyone pays attention to you.

Headman (flattered): Yes, yes, they do. They do, or else.

Amal: Do the Raja's messengers listen to you, too?

Headman: Of course! Would they dare to ignore me?

Amal: Will you tell the messengers that my name is Amal, and that I am always here, sitting by the window?

Headman: Why should I do that?

Amal: In case there is a letter addressed to me.

Headman: A letter for you! Who would write *you* a letter?

Amal: If the Raja writes to me then—

Headman: Well now, aren't you a mighty fellow! Ho ho ho! So the Raja will write to you, will he? Of course he will, for you are his dear friend. In fact, he's getting sadder by the day because he's not seen you lately, so I hear. Well, your waiting's almost over; I bet that your letter will come any day now.

Amal: Mr. Headman, why is your voice so harsh? Are you angry with me?

Headman: Goodness me. Why should I be angry with you? Could I be so bold? After all, you are a correspondent of the Raja. *(aside)* I can see that Madhav Dutta thinks he can drop the names of rajas and maharajas, just because he has made a little money. We'll soon see that he gets his comeuppance— Yes, my lad, you'll soon get a royal letter at your house, I shall see to it myself.

Amal: No no, please, you don't have to go to any trouble for me.

Headman: And why not? I will tell our Raja about you, and I am sure he will not keep you waiting long. In fact, I bet he will send a footman at once to hear your news. *(aside)* Really, Madhav Dutta's arrogance is too much. Just as soon as this reaches the ears of the Raja, there'll be trouble, that's for sure.

[he goes]

Amal: Who is that, with her jingling anklets? Please stop awhile.

a girl enters

Girl: How can I stop? The day's already passing.

Amal: You don't want to stop, even for a moment—and I don't want to sit here a moment longer.

Girl: To look at you reminds me of the fading morning star. What's the matter with you, tell me?

Amal: I don't know, but the doctor has forbidden me to go out.

Girl: Then don't go out, obey Doctor's words—if you don't, people will say you are naughty. I can see that just looking outside makes you restless. Let me close this window a bit.

Amal: No no, don't close it! Everything is closed to me except this window. Tell me who you are, I don't seem to know you.

Girl: I am Shudha.

Amal: Shudha?

Shudha: Don't you know? I am the daughter of the local flower seller.

Amal: And what do you do?

Shudha: I fill a wicker basket with plucked flowers and make garlands. Just now I'm off to pick some.

Amal: You're going to pick flowers? Is that why your feet are so lively, and your anklets go *jingle-jangle* with each step? If I

could go with you, I would pick flowers for you from the highest branches, beyond your sight.

Shudha: Would you now?! So you know where the flowers are better than I do?

Amal: Yes, I know a lot. For example, I know all about the seven *champak*-flower brothers. If I were well, I would go deep into the forest where there is no path to be seen. There I would blossom as a *champak* flower on the tallest tip of the thinnest twig, where the hummingbird gets drunk on honey. Will you be Parul, my *champak*-flower sister?

Shudha: How silly! How could I be your Parul *didi*? I am Shudha, daughter of Shashi, the flower seller. Everyday I have to string many flower garlands. If I could spend the day sitting like you, then I would be very happy.

Amal: What would you do if you had all day?

Shudha: First, I would play with my *bene-bou* doll and marry her off, and then there's my pussycat, Meni. I would love to—but it's getting late, and there won't be any flowers left if I dawdle here.

Amal: Please talk to me a little longer, I'm enjoying it.

Shudha: All right, if you are a good boy and stay here quietly, on my way back with the flowers I'll stop for another chat.

Amal: Will you bring me a flower?

Shudha: How can I? Can you pay?

Amal: I'll pay you when I grow up, when I've gone out seeking work beyond the stream over there—then I'll repay you.

Shudha: I accept.

Amal: So you will return after picking flowers?

Shudha: I will return.

Amal: Promise?

Shudha: I promise.

Amal: You won't forget me? My name is Amal. Will you remember it?

Shudha: No, I won't forget. You will be remembered.

[she goes]

some boys enter

Amal: Brothers, where are you going? Stop for a while.

Boys: We're off to play.

Amal: What game are you going to play?

Boys: The ploughman's game.

First boy (waving a stick): This is our ploughshare.

Second boy: And we two will be the oxen.

Amal: Will you play all day?

Boys: Yes, the entire day.

Amal: After that, will you come back home along the path by the river?

A boy: Yes, we will, when it's evening.

Amal: Please drop by here, in front of my house.

A boy: You can come with us now, come and play.

Amal: Doctor's ordered me not to go out.

A boy: Doctor! Why do you listen to him? Come on, let's go, it's getting late.

Amal: Please, friends, won't you play in the road outside my window, just for a little while?

A boy: But there's nothing here to play with.

Amal: All my toys are lying right here, take them all. It's no fun playing indoors all alone—the toys are just lying here, doing nothing, scattered in the dust.

Boys: Oh, what wonderful toys! Look at this ship! And this one with the matted hair is the old witch, Jatai. And here's a terrific *sepoy* to play soldiers with. Are you really giving us these? Won't you miss them?

Amal: No, I won't miss them, you can have them all.

A boy: So we don't have to give them back?

Amal: No, you don't need to.

A boy: Nobody will scold you?

Amal: No, nobody will. But promise me that you will come and play with them outside my house for a while each morning. When they get worn out, I'll get you some new ones.

A boy: All right, friend, we'll come and play here every day. Now let's take the *sepoys* and have a battle. Where can we get muskets? Over there, there's a large piece of reed—that'll do if we cut it up into pieces. But friend, you are dozing off!

Amal: Yes, I'm very sleepy. Why I feel sleepy so often, I don't know. But I've been sitting up a long time and I can't sit any longer; my back is aching.

A boy: It's only the beginning of the day—why are you sleepy already? Listen, there goes the gong.

Amal: Yes—*dhong dhong dhong*; it lulls me to sleep.

Boys: We're going now, but we'll be back in the morning.

Amal: Before you go, let me ask you something. You go about a lot. Do you know the Raja's messengers?

Boys: Yes we do, quite well.

Amal: Who are they? What are their names?

Boys: One's called Badal, another's called Sharat, and there are others.

Amal: Well, if a letter comes for me, will they know who I am?

A boy: Why not? If your name is on the letter, they will certainly find you.

Amal: When you come back in the morning, please ask one of them to stop by and meet me, will you?

Boys: Yes, we will.

◈ *Act Three* ◈

Amal, in bed

Amal: Uncle, can't I even sit near the window today? Doctor really forbids it?

Madhav: Yes, he does. He says that sitting there every day is making your illness worse.

Amal: But Uncle, that's not right—I don't know about my illness, but I know I feel better when I sit there.

Madhav: Sitting there you have become friends with half the town—young and old alike. The area outside my door looks like a fairground. How will you stand the strain? Look at your face today—so wan!

Amal: If my friend the fakir comes by my window, he will miss me and go away again.

Madhav: Who is this fakir?

Amal: Every day he drops in and tells me tales of lands far and wide; he's so much fun to listen to.

Madhav: I don't know of any fakir.

Amal: He usually comes along about now. Uncle, I beg you, please ask him to come and sit with me.

Thakurda enters, dressed as a fakir

Amal: There you are, Fakir. Come and sit on my bed.

Madhav: What! Is that your—

Thakurda (winking): I am the fakir.

Madhav: Of course you are.

Amal: Where have you been this time, Fakir?

Thakurda: To the Island of Parrots. I just got back.

Madhav: Parrot Island, eh?

Thakurda: Why so skeptical? Am I like you? When I travel, there are no expenses. I can go wherever I please.

Amal (clapping in delight): You have so much fun. When I get well, you promised I could be your disciple, remember?

Thakurda: Of course. I will initiate you in my travel *mantras*, so that neither ocean nor mountain nor forest will bar your way.

Madhav: What is all this crazy talk?

Thakurda: Dearest Amal, there is nothing in mountain or ocean that frightens me—but if the doctor and your uncle get together, my *mantras* will be powerless.

Amal: You won't tell Doctor about all of this, will you Uncle? Now I promise I will lie here, sleep and do nothing. But the day I get well I will swear by Fakir's *mantras*, and then I shall cross the rivers, mountains, and oceans.

Madhav: Hush, son, don't keep on talking about leaving—just to hear you makes me feel so sad.

Amal: Tell me, Fakir, what is Parrot Island like?

Thakurda: It's a rather weird place, a land of birds without any human beings. The birds do not speak or come to land, they only sing and fly around.

Amal: How fantastic! And is there ocean all around?

Thakurda: Yes, of course.

Amal: And are there green hills?

Thakurda: Yes, in the hills, the birds make their nests. In the evening, as the rays of the setting sun make the green hillsides glow, the parrots flock to their nests in a green swarm—and then the hills and the parrots become one single mass of green. It's indescribable.

Amal: And what about streams and waterfalls?

Thakurda: Absolutely! How could there not be?! They flow like molten diamonds, and how the drops dance! The small pebbles in the streams hum and murmur as the waters gush over them, until finally they plunge into the ocean. No one, not even a doctor, can restrain them for even a single second. I tell you, if the birds did not ostracize me as a mere man, I would make myself a small hut among the thousands of nests beside some waterfall and pass my days watching the waters and the ocean waves below.

Amal: If I were a bird then—

Thakurda: Then there would be a problem. I hear you have already arranged with the *daiwallah* to sell *dai* when you grow up. I don't think your business would do too well among parrots. Who knows, you might even take a loss.

Madhav: I can't take this nonsense any longer! You two will drive me crazy. I am going.

Amal: Uncle, has my *daiwallah* come and gone yet?

Madhav: Of course he has. He won't make ends meet by carrying things for you and your fancy fakir friend, or by flitting around Parrot Island, will he? But he left a pot of *dai* for you, and he said to tell you that his youngest niece is getting married in his village—so he's rather busy, because he has to go and book the flute players from Kalmipara.

Amal: But he promised that his youngest niece would marry me.

Thakurda: Now we *are* in trouble.

Amal: He said she would be a delicious bride, with a nose ring and a red-striped sari. With her own hands she would milk a black cow in the mornings and bring me an earthenware bowl full of frothy, fresh milk. And at evening time, after taking a lamp to the cowshed, she would settle down with me and tell me tales of the seven *champak*-flower brothers.

Thakurda: Well, she sounds like a wonderful bride. Even a fakir like me feels tempted. But don't lose heart, my child, let him marry off this niece. I give you my word that when your time comes, there will be no shortage of nieces in his family.

Madhav: Be off with you! This time you really have gone too far.

[Madhav goes]

Amal: Fakir, now that Uncle's gone, tell me secretly—has the Raja sent a letter in my name to the post office?

Thakurda: I hear that his letter has been dispatched—it is on its way.

Amal: On its way? Which way? Is it coming by that path through the dense forest that you see when the sky clears after rain?

Thakurda: Yes. You seem to know it.

Amal: I know a lot, Fakir.

Thakurda: So I see—but how?

Amal: I can't say. I can see everything before my eyes, as if I have really seen it many times, but long ago—how long ago I cannot recall. Shall I describe it to you? I can see the Raja's messenger coming down the hillside alone, a lantern in his left hand and on his back a bag of letters, descending for days and nights; and then at the foot of the hills, where the waterfall becomes a winding stream, he follows the footpath along the bank and walks on through the corn; then comes the sugar-cane field and he disappears into the narrow lane that cuts through the tall stems of sugarcanes; and then he reaches the open meadow where the cricket chirps and where there is no one to be seen, only the snipe wagging their tails and poking at the mud with their beaks. I can picture it all. And the nearer he gets, the gladder I feel.

Thakurda: Though I do not have your fresh vision, still I see it.

Amal: Tell me, Fakir, do you know the Raja?

Thakurda: I certainly do. I often go to his court to seek alms.

Amal: Really? When I get better I will go with you and seek alms from him. Can I go with you?

Thakurda: Son, you do not need to seek—he will give without your asking.

Amal: But I would rather seek. I'll go to the road outside his palace chanting "Victory to the Raja!" and begging alms—maybe I will also dance with a cymbal. What do you think?

Thakurda: It sounds good; and if I accompany you, I will receive gifts, too. What will you ask him for?

Amal: I will ask him to make me a Raja's messenger, who will go all over the land with a lantern in his hand delivering messages from door to door. You know, Fakir, someone has told me that as soon as I am well, he will teach me how to beg. I will go out begging with him wherever I please.

Thakurda: And who is this person?

Amal: Chidam.

Thakurda: Which Chidam?

Amal: Blind and lame Chidam. Every day he comes to my window. A boy just like me pushes him around in a cart with wheels. I've often told Chidam that when I'm better, I will push him around, too.

Thakurda: That would be interesting, I can see.

Amal: He is going to teach me all about begging. I tell Uncle that we should give Chidam something, but Uncle says that he's not really blind or lame. Perhaps he is not totally blind, but I know he does not see very well—I am sure of that.

Thakurda: You are right. Whether you call him blind or not, it is true that he does not see very well. But if he gets no alms from you, why does he like to sit with you?

Amal: Because he hears all about different places from me. The poor fellow cannot see, but he listens when I tell him about all the lands that you tell me about. The other day you told me of the Land of No Weight, where everything weighs nothing and even a tiny hop will send you sailing over a hill. He really liked hearing about that place. Fakir, how do you reach that land?

Thakurda: There's an inner road, but it's hard to find.

Amal: Since the poor man is blind, he will never see any

place, and will have to go on begging alms. Sometimes he moans to me about it, and I tell him that at least he visits a lot of places as a beggar—not everyone can do that.

Thakurda: Son, why do you feel so sad to stay at home?

Amal: Not sad, not now. Until now, my days did drag endlessly—but I have seen the Raja's post office and I am happier. I even like sitting indoors. I know my letter will come, and the thought keeps me company, so I wait quite happily. But I have no idea what the Raja will write in his letter.

Thakurda: You do not need to know. As long as your name is there, that is enough.

Madhav enters

Madhav: Do you two realize what trouble you have gotten us into?

Thakurda: Why, what's up?

Madhav: Rumor has it that you are saying that the Raja has built his post office only to correspond with you.

Thakurda: So?

Madhav: And so the Headman has sent an anonymous letter about this to the Raja.

Thakurda: We all know that most things reach the Raja's ears.

Madhav: Then why didn't you watch yourself? Why did you take the names of rajas and maharajas in vain?! You'll pull me in, too.

Amal: Fakir, will the Raja be angry?

Thakurda: Who says so? Why should he be? How can he rule his kingdom with majesty if he becomes mad at a child like you and a fakir like me?

Amal: You know, Fakir, since this morning there has been a kind of darkness in my mind; sometimes things look as if in a dream. I feel like being totally silent. I don't want to talk anymore. Won't the Raja's letter ever come? Just now, this room seemed to vanish, as if everything—as if all . . .

Thakurda (fanning Amal): It will come, my dear, the letter will come today.

Doctor enters

Doctor: So how do you feel today?

Amal: Doctor, I am now feeling comfortable; all my pain seems to be going away.

Doctor (aside to Madhav): I don't like the look of that smile very much. When he says he feels better there is danger in store. As the great Chakradhar Dutta says—

Madhav: *Please* Doctor, spare me Chakradhar Dutta. Just tell me, what is the matter?

Doctor: It looks as if we cannot hold onto him much longer. I recommended certain precautions, but he seems to have been exposed to the outside air.

Madhav: No, Doctor, I have done my utmost to keep him from such exposure. He has been kept indoors, and most of the time the place was kept shut.

Doctor: The air has turned rather strange today, and I notice a severe draft blowing through your door. That is not at all good. You must shut the door at once. Try not to have any visitors for a few days. If people drop in, they can come through the back door. And you should get rid of this glare that comes through the window when the sun sets—it disturbs the patient's mind.

Madhav: Amal's eyes are closed. I think he's asleep. When I look at his face, it's as if—oh Doctor! this child who is not my own but whom I have loved as my own, will he be taken from me?

Doctor: Who's coming now? It's the Headman, coming here. Drat! I must go, my friend. Go inside and shut your door tight. When I get home, I'll send over a strong dose—give it to the boy. If he can resist its power, he may yet pull through.

[Doctor and Madhav go]

Headman enters

Headman: Hey, boy!

Thakurda (suddenly standing up): Ssh ssh . . . be quiet!

Amal: No, Fakir, you thought I was sleeping, but I wasn't. I heard everything. And I also heard faraway talk; my parents were talking beside my bed.

Madhav enters

Headman: So, Madhav Dutta, these days you are rubbing shoulders with people in high places!

Madhav: What do you mean, Headman? Don't make fun of us. We are very humble folk.

Headman: But isn't your boy awaiting a letter from the Raja?

Madhav: He's a mere child, and sick and confused at that. Why do you listen to him?

Headman: On the contrary. Where else could our Raja find a worthier correspondent than your boy? That must be why he has built his new royal post office outside your window. Hey little fellow, there is a letter from the Raja addressed to you.

Amal (startled): Really?

Headman: And why not?—with your royal friendship! *(hands him a blank sheet)* Ha ha ha, here's your letter.

Amal: Are you teasing? Fakir, Fakir, tell me, is it really the letter?

Thakurda: Yes, my boy, you have your Fakir's word, it is indeed the letter.

Amal: But my eyes can't see anything—everything looks blank to me! Headman, sir, tell me what's in the letter.

Headman: His Majesty writes, "I will be visiting your home shortly. Prepare me a meal of puffed rice and parched paddy with molasses. I don't like to stay in the palace one minute more than I have to." Ha ha ha!

Madhav (with folded hands): I beg you, Sir, I implore you, do not ridicule us.

Thakurda: Ridicule! What ridicule? Who would dare to ridicule!

Madhav: What! Thakurda, are you out of your mind?

Thakurda: Maybe I am. But I also see letters on this sheet. The Raja writes that he will personally visit Amal, and that his royal physician will accompany him.

Amal: Fakir—it is true! I hear his herald! Can you hear the call?

Headman: Ha ha ha! Let him become a bit more demented, then he'll hear it!

Amal: Headman, Sir, I thought that you were angry with me, that you disliked me. I never imagined that you would bring me the Raja's letter—it never occurred to me. I must wash the dust from your feet.

Headman: Well, I'll say this much, the boy certainly has good manners. Not too bright, but he has a good heart.

Amal: The day is nearly over, I can feel it. There goes the evening gong—*dhong dhong dhong, dhong dhong dhong*. Has the evening star appeared yet, Fakir? Why don't I see it?

Thakurda: They have shut all your windows. I will open them.

a banging at the outside door

Madhav: What's that! Who's there? What an annoyance!

(from outside): Open the door.

Madhav: Who are you?

(from outside): Open the door.

Madhav: Headman, could it be robbers?

Headman: Who's there? This is Panchanan Morhal, Headman, speaking. Aren't you scared? *(to Madhav)* Listen! The banging has stopped. Even the toughest thieves know to fear Panchanan's voice!

Madhav (looking out the window): Look! They have smashed the door, that's why the banging has ceased!

Raja's herald enters

Raja's herald: His Majesty will arrive tonight.

Headman: Disaster!

Amal: When in the night, Herald? At what hour?

Herald: In the dead of night.

Amal: When my friend the watchman strikes his gong at the town's Lion Gate, *dhong dhong dhong, dhong dhong dhong*—at that hour?

Herald: Yes, at that hour. In the meantime, the Raja has sent his finest physician to attend to his little friend.

Raja's physician enters

Raja's physician: What's this? All closed up?! Open up, open up, open all the doors and windows. *(he feels Amal's body)* How are you feeling, young fellow?

Amal: Quite well, very well, Doctor. My illness is gone, my pain is gone. Now everything is open—I can see all the stars, shining on the far side of darkness.

Physician: When the Raja comes in the dead of night, will you rise and go forth with him?

Amal: I will, I have the will. I long to go forth. I will ask the Raja to show me the Pole Star in the heavens. Perhaps I have seen it many times, and have not recognized it.

Physician: The Raja will show you all things. *(to Madhav)* Please make the room clean and decorate it with flowers to greet our Raja. *(pointing to the Headman)* That man should not be permitted here.

Amal: Oh no, Doctor, he is my friend. Before you came, he brought me the Raja's letter.

Physician: All right, my boy, since he is your friend, he may remain.

Madhav (whispering in Amal's ear): My son, the Raja loves you, and he is coming here in person. Please entreat him to give us something. You know our condition—we are not well off.

Amal: Uncle, I have already thought about it—do not worry.

Madhav: What will you request?

Amal: I will beg him to make me a royal messenger in his post office. I will deliver his messages to homes everywhere.

Madhav (striking his forehead): Alas, such is my fate!

Amal: Uncle, when the Raja comes, what shall we offer him?

Herald: The Raja has commanded a meal of puffed rice and parched paddy with molasses.

Amal: Headman, those were your very words! You knew everything about the Raja, and we knew nothing!

Headman: If you would send someone to my house, we will endeavor to provide his Majesty with good—

Physician: No need for it. Now you must all be calm. It is coming, coming, his sleep is coming. I will sit beside his pillow as he drifts off. Blow out the lamp; let the starlight come in; his sleep has arrived.

Madhav (to Thakurda): Thakurda, why so hushed, with your palms pressed together like a statue? I feel a kind of dread. These do not seem like good omens. Why has the room been darkened? What use is starlight?

Thakurda: Be quiet, unbeliever! Do not speak.

Shudha enters

Shudha: Amal?

Physician: He has fallen asleep.

Shudha: I have brought flowers for him. Can I put them in his hand?

Physician: Yes, you may give him your flowers.

Shudha: When will he awake?

Physician: When the Raja comes and calls him.

Shudha: Will you whisper a word in his ear for me?

Physician: What shall I say?

Shudha: Tell him, "Shudha has not forgotten you."

Glossary

◈

Ayurveda ancient system of medicine recorded in the *Vedas*, the oldest writings of India.

bene-bou (doll) commonest type of clay doll in rural Bengal.

champak species of magnolia, well-known in Bengali folk literature.

chhatu fine flour made of maize, barley, etc.

dai (dahi) curds.

daiwallah curdseller.

didi elder sister.

fakir Hindu or Muslim ascetic, holy man.

mantra symbol, word, or phrase used in meditation, believed to possess spiritual powers; it is generally given by a guru to his *chela* (disciple).

parul species of trumpet-flower, well-known in Bengali folk literature.

Ramayana one of the two ancient epics of India, the other being the *Mahabharata*.

sepoy native Indian soldier under European, especially British, discipline.

sloka couplet or verse, taken from classical or folk literature.

About the Author

◈

RABINDRANATH TAGORE (1861–1941) was awarded the Nobel prize for literature in 1913, the first Asian writer so honored. Widely regarded as the greatest modern Indian writer, Tagore was also an accomplished song composer and painter. An educational and social reformer on a par with Gandhi, Tagore was one of the very first to perceive that East and West would be compelled to meet in the twentieth century, a theme taken up in many of his works. His most spiritually moving work and his only play that is still regularly performed outside Bengal, *The Post Office* served as inspiration to the children of the Warsaw ghetto and was read over French radio in André Gide's translation the night before the Nazis seized Paris.

About the Translators

KRISHNA DUTTA, who was born and raised in Calcutta, now lives in London, where she works as a teacher. She is the translator of *Selected Short Stories* by Rabindranath Tagore, and *Glimpses of Bengal*, a collection of letters written by Tagore to his niece. She is also the author of *Rabindranath Tagore: The Myriad-Minded Man*, which she cowrote with Andrew Robinson.

ANDREW ROBINSON is literary editor of *The Times Higher Education Supplement*. A graduate of Oxford, he has traveled extensively in India and Bengal since 1975. He is the author of *Satyajit Ray: The Inner Eye, The Art of Rabindranath Tagore*, and *Rabindranath Tagore: The Myriad-Minded Man*, which he cowrote with Krishna Dutta. He lives in London.

About the Illustrator

MICHAEL McCURDY, the well-known illustrator and woodcut artist, lives in Great Barrington, Massachusetts. He has illustrated numerous books, among them *Passover*, by David Mamet.